Frank L. Stanton

Songs of a day and songs of the the soil

Frank L. Stanton

Songs of a day and songs of the the soil

ISBN/EAN: 9783743323292

Manufactured in Europe, USA, Canada, Australia, Japa

Cover: Foto ©Andreas Hilbeck / pixelio.de

Manufactured and distributed by brebook publishing software
(www.brebook.com)

Frank L. Stanton

Songs of a day and songs of the the soil

SONGS OF A DAY

AND

SONGS OF THE SOIL

BY

FRANK L. STANTON

——

NEW YORK
JOHN B. ALDEN, PUBLISHER
1892

INTRODUCTION.

THIS collection of Mr. Stanton's poems and songs is put forth neither as an experiment nor as a bid for the passing notoriety which in these days is sometimes mistaken for fame. It is issued in response to a demand which has come from all parts of the country—not a popular demand, but requests and suggestions from friends, strangers, and the press.

That these poems have touched a popular chord is shown by the fact that they have been widely copied in the newspapers. Some of the pieces have been set to music, and in this shape have attracted wide attention. To my mind, the melody that is native to them is their finest setting.

It should be said, not by way of apology, but by way of explanation, that the poems in this little volume are the flowers that have sprung up in the wilderness of daily newspaper work, blooming unexpectedly, even to the author, between paragraphs or side by side with the results of the most arduous routine work.

From the beginning of the book to the end, the reader will not find an artificial note. Sincerity and simplicity prevail throughout. Surely there is a touch of originality in the fact that the poet, with such remarkable facility for rhyme and metre and in the outward forms of his art, should cling so persistently to what is simple and true.

JOEL CHANDLER HARRIS.

ATLANTA, GA., January 1, 1892.

CONTENTS.

CONTENTS.

CONTENTS. vi

SONGS OF A DAY.

THE LOVE UNKNOWN.

Sweetheart, you have not known me,—
   If I be great or wise;
Yet somewhere you shall own me
   Beneath God's splendid skies;
Though now life's broken chalice
   No earthly sweets can win,
Some day, at Love's own palace,
   Your arms shall take me in!

Some day a rose will blossom
   White in the thorny ways,
And on the dark Night's bosom
   Will fall the morning's rays;
Some day when I am lying
   Pale from the storm and strife,
Your lips shall seek me, dying,
   And kiss me back to life!

Then will the bird-songs, ringing,
   Fall soft on fields of bloom;
Then will the streams flow singing
   Through groves of rich perfume!

Then shall the world benighted,
  The rarest splendor win,
And at Love's palace lighted
  Your arms shall take me in!

CLARISSE.

Kiss you?   Wherefore should I, sweet?
  Casual kissing I condemn;
Other lips your lips will meet
  When my kisses die on them.
Should I grieve that this should be?
Nay, if you will kiss, kiss me!

Love you?   That were vainer still!
  If you win my love to-day,
When the morrow comes you will
  Lightly laugh that love away.
Should I grieve that this should be?
Nay, if you must love, love me.

Wherefore play these fickle parts?
  Life and love will soon be done.
Think you God made human hearts
  Just for you to tread upon?
Will you break them, nor repine?
If you will, Clarisse, break mine!

MY STUDY.

The day in the west has faded,
  And night with auroral bars
The brow of the north has braided
  And brightened the blue with stars;
And here in the firelight ruddy,
  In this temple of mystic art
Which I modestly call "My study,"
  I'm writing to you, sweetheart.

I wish you could see me bending
  Over my books sublime,
And drearily, wearily wending
  My way through the realms of rhyme!
I have sixteen songs and a sonnet
  Just finished (my stock in trade),
And a verse, "On a Lady's Bonnet,"
  Which will come too high, I'm afraid.

The room where I write is cheerful
  And warm—when it isn't cold;
But its objects of art are fearful
  And wonderful to behold!
There's a chimney with grate of iron,
  Where the flaming firelight throws
Its gleam on a bust of Byron,
  And a Cæsar with broken nose!

Then a bird on a bust of Pallas,
    The Raven of Edgar Poe,
Looks down from the mantel callous
    To the years as they come and go.
On a desk are the works of Schiller,
   . And Goethe, in bindings plain;
The songs of Joaquin Miller
    And the poems of Paul H. Hayne.

Then Homer, the famed old Grecian,
    With an aspect devoid of joy,
In a binding old (Venetian),
    Comes next with the Siege of Troy.
(Alas! had the great bard ever
    Dreamed of this destiny sad,
He'd have burned what he wrote, or never
    Penned a line of the Iliad!)

I sometimes think that the Muses
    Grow thin in this Attic air;
But we live as our fortune chooses,
    And Fortune has left me here.
I am used to her pranks and capers,
    But well does she act her part;
She gives me my books and papers
    And a kiss from your lips, sweetheart!

LOVE'S RECOMPENSE.

Beneath the shroud the dead man lay
   And dreamed not that his love drew near;
But on his heart there fell that day—
   And angels saw it fall—a tear.

When lo! above the barren sod,
   By never any sunshine lit,
A white, sweet rose looked up to God,
   And God looked down and smiled on it!

LYNCHED.

The tramp of horse adown a sullen glen;
Dark forms of stern, unmerciful masked
   men.

A clash of arms, a cloven prison door,
And a man's cry for mercy! . . . Then high
   o'er

The barren fields, dim outlined in the storm,
The swaying of a lifeless human form.

And close beside, in horror and affright,
A widowed woman wailing to the night.

A LITTLE HAND.

Perhaps there are tenderer, sweeter things
  Somewhere in this sun-bright land;
But I thank the Lord for His blessings,
  And the clasp of a little hand.

A little hand that softly stole
  Into my own that day,
When I needed the touch that I loved so much
  To strengthen me on the way.

Softer it seemed than the softest down
  On the breast of the gentlest dove;
But its timid press and its faint caress
  Were strong in the strength of love!

It seemed to say in a strange, sweet way:
  "I love you and understand;"
And calmed my fears as my hot, heart tears
  Fell over that little hand.

        .   .   .   .   .   .

Perhaps there are tenderer, sweeter things
  Somewhere in this sun-bright land;
But I thank the Lord for His blessings,
  And the clasp of a little hand.

A LITTLE WAY.

A little way to walk with you, my own—
    Only a little way,
Then one of us must weep and walk alone
    Until God's day.

A little way! It is so sweet to live
    Together, that I know
Life would not have one withered rose to give
    If one of us should go.

And if these lips should ever learn to smile,
    With your heart far from mine,
'Twould be for joy that in a little while
    They would be kissed by thine!

THE TOILER.

Heavy the heart and weary the brain,
    But write, my pen, oh, write!
For rest from labor will come again,
    With a kiss from her lips at night.

Sonnet and story—trace them well,
    In beautiful lines and bright;
But the tenderest thought in my heart will
      dwell
    On the kiss from her lips at night.

And the world may frown on the head
    bowed down,
  And its splendors veil from sight;
I bear the cross, for I gain the crown
    With a kiss from her lips at night!

A GHOST.

All night beside my dreamless bed
She walks with soft and thrilling tread—
Living through death and all things dead.

She does not speak—a form of mist,
Holding with life a solemn tryst,
With hands unclasped and lips unkissed.

But could I touch those lips and feel
The white, sweet arms about me steal;
Though Death did then his face reveal

And flash his sword between us—I,
Mad in that moment's ecstasy,
Would kiss her heavenly lips and die!

WEARY THE WAITING.

There's an end to all toiling some day—
    sweet day,
  (But it's weary the waiting, weary!)
There's a harbor somewhere in a peaceful
    bay
Where the sails will be furled and the ship
    will lay
At anchor—somewhere in the far-away—
  (But it's weary the waiting, weary!)

There's an end to the troubles of souls
    opprest,
  (But it's weary the waiting, weary!)
Some time in the future when God thinks
    best,
He'll lay us tenderly down to rest,
And roses'll grow from the thorns in the
    breast.
  (But it's weary the waiting, weary!)

There's an end to the world with its stormy
    frown,
  (But it's weary the waiting, weary!)
There's a light somewhere that no dark can
    drown,

And where life's sad burdens are all laid
    down,
A crown—thank God!—for each cross—a
    crown!
    (But it's weary the waiting, weary!)

A LOVE NOTE.

Do not forget me, dearest; all day long
    I think of you, and wish the time more fleet;
My heart is always singing some sweet song,
    And thinking of you makes my labor
      sweet.
And if the day seems anywise less bright—
    More vext with cares than I had thought
      'twould be—
I think with joy of the approaching night
    When the sweet stars shall guide my steps
      to thee.
One thought still whispers—sweeter ever-
      more:
"Thou shalt behold her when the day is
      o'er!"

And so I shall; for you will watch and wait
    When on the flowers the tears of twilight
      fall;
Sweet are the roses 'round your garden gate,
    But you are still the sweetest rose of all!

And you are my rose—even my very own,
  And to my life your beauty you impart;
Bloom sweetly still, but bloom for me alone,
  And twine your tendrils closer 'round my
    heart.
Dear, I shall soon within your presence be,
And you are waiting with a kiss for me!

A LOVE SONG.

Sweetheart, there is no splendor
  In all God's splendid skies
Bright as the love-light tender
  That dwells in your dear eyes!

Sweetheart, there are no blisses
  Like those thy lips distil;
Of all the world's sweet kisses
  Thy kiss is sweetest still!

Sweetheart, no white dove flying
  Had e'er as soft a breast
As this sweet hand that's lying
  Clasped in my own—at rest!

Sweetheart, there is no glory
  That clusters 'round my life
Bright as this bright, sweet story:
  "My sweetheart and my wife!"

THE REAPERS.

The wind is soft in the waving wheat,
  With a sigh for the maids who love us;
The hives are heavy with honey, sweet
  As the lips of the maids   ho love us.
    Oh, reapers, sing
    As your keen blades ring,
As blithe as the birds above us!
    The golden crown
    Of the wheat bends down
At the feet of the maids who love us.

Here's gold for them in the golden wheat
  Which the palms that we press shall cover;
But a lass that loves with a true heart's beat
  Asks only love of her lover.
    Then, reapers, sing
    As your keen blades ring,
Till the stars peep out above us;
    And the twilight thrills
    With the whippoorwills
Calling home to the hearts that love us!

AT THE GRAVE OF PAUL H. HAYNE.

Where the winds their clamors cease,
Where the dewy flowers of peace
Sweeten through the grassy sod
And the silence breathes of God;
Sweet he sleeps whose songs were sweet,
And I pause with reverent feet
As I lay upon his shrine
This poor, withered wreath of mine!

Withered, but each leaflet bears
The soft imprint of my tears!
Tears from eyes his death made dim—
Tears that fall for love of him;
For I loved his songs, and they
Sing themselves to me to-day,
Till I feel and see him near—
Not in dust and daisies there!

With the laurel on his brow,
Sings the Master sweeter now;
And his loftier numbers rise
Mid the palms of Paradise!
Still, when twilight steals apace
And the veil on Heaven's face

Twinkles through with stars, I seem
Listening still, as in a dream,
To the melody that floats
From his last sweet earthly notes!
Notes that blend at morn and even
With the songs he sings in Heaven!

AT LAST.

Oh, the sights that he had seen
  In the far and travelled lands!
His heart was cold and the sword was keen
  In his merciless, reckless hands.

And never a foe he spared—
  No pangs for the lives he slew;
And never a God in the heavens he feared,
  Though God looked on and knew!

But God was wiser still;
  Love conquers hate and pride;
His shafts are keen to heal or kill,
  And at Love's feet he died!

LITTLE ELAINE.

Where have you gone, little Elaine,
With the eyes like violets wet with rain—
Silvery April rain that throws
Melting diamonds over the rose?
(Ah, never were eyes as bright as those!)
You have left me alone; but where have you
       flown?
God knows, my dear, God knows!

Where have you gone, little Elaine,
With laughing lips of the crimson stain—
Lips that smiled as the sunlight glows
When morning breaks like a white, sweet
       rose
Over the wearisome winter snows?
Shall I miss their song my whole life long?
God knows, my dear, God knows!

You have left me lonely, little Elaine:
I call to you, but I call in vain;
I sing to you when the twilight throws
Its dying light on my life's last rose,
While the tide of Memory ebbs and flows.
Is it God's own will I should miss you still?
God knows, my dear, God knows!

THE MASTER'S COMING.

In a desolate night and lonely, afar in a
    desolate land,
I waited the Master's coming—the touch of
    His healing hand.
The gates of His house were guarded and
    sealed with a seal of stone,
Yet still for His steps I waited and wept in
    the dark alone.

And I said: "When the guards are dream-
    ing I will steal to His couch of rest;
He will think of my weary vigils and wel-
    come me to His breast."
But lo! when the seal was broken, the couch
    where my Master lay
Held only His shining garments—they had
    taken my Lord away!

Then my soul in its grief and anguish lay
    down in the dark to die
Under a hopeless heaven, under a sunless
    sky;
But my dreams were all of the Master—dear
    as my soul was dear,
And waking, I saw the glory of His beauti-
    ful presence there!

And He said, as I fell and worshipped:
"Arise, and the Master see;
Behold the thorns that have crowned Him—
the wounds that were made for thee!"

.   .   .   .

I wait for the Master's coming now as in
days gone by,
Under a hopeful heaven, under a cloudless
sky;
And still when the guards are dreaming I
steal to His couch of rest;
His smile through the darkness lightens, and
welcomes me to His breast!

SAINT MICHAEL'S BELLS.

I wonder if the bells ring now, as in the days
of old,
From the solemn star-crowned tower with
the glittering cross of gold;
The tower that overlooks the sea whose shin-
ing bosom swells
To the ringing and the singing of sweet
Saint Michael's bells?

I have heard them in the morning when the
mists gloomed cold and gray
O'er the distant walls of Sumter looking
seaward from the bay,

And at twilight I have listened to the musi-
cal farewells
That came flying, sighing, dying from sweet
Saint Michael's bells.

Great joy it was to hear them, for they sang
sweet songs to me
Where the sheltered ships rocked gently in
the haven—safe from sea,
And the captains and the sailors heard no
more the ocean's knells,
But thanked God for home and loved ones
and sweet Saint Michael's bells.

They seemed to waft a welcome across the
ocean's foam
To all the lost and lonely: "Come home—
come home—come home!
Come home, where skies are brighter—
where love still yearning dwells!"
So sang the bells in music—the sweet Saint
Michael's bells!

They are ringing now as ever. But I know
that not for me
Shall the bells of sweet Saint Michael's ring
welcome o'er the sea;

I have knelt within their shadow, where my
    heart still dreams and dwells,
But I'll hear no more the music of sweet
    Saint Michael's bells.

Oh, ring, sweet bells, forever, an echo in my
    breast
Soft as a mother's voice that lulls a loved one
    into rest!
Ring welcome to the hearts at home—to me
    your sad farewells
When I sleep the last sleep, dreaming of
    sweet Saint Michael's bells!

AT ANDERSONVILLE.

When the weird, wondering wind is still,
There, in the valleys at Andersonville,
At that shivering hour—the grim half-way
Of the ghostly march of the dark to day,
There are sounds too mystical to repeat;
Eager voices, hurrying feet,
Ribald laughter and jest—and then
The prayers and pleadings of 'prisoned men.

At dead of night, when the wind is still,
There is life in the shadows at Andersonville.

When the hills gloom black in the midnight
    shade
There are signs of life in the old stockade;
The phantom guards in the prison bounds
Resume their sorrowful, silent rounds;
While the glow-worm's lantern gleams and
    waves
Adown the aisles of a thousand graves;
And then to the listening ear there comes
The mystic roll of the muffled drums.

The drama ends and the dreamer wakes;
In the flowering fields and tangled brakes
The birds are singing; the liquid notes
Rise to heaven from their thrilling throats;
The sunlight falls with a softened beam
On the voiceless graves where the dead men
    dream;
While hill and valley and prison sod
Rest in the smile and the peace of God.

But at dead of night, when the wind is still,
There is life in the shadows at Andersonville.

THE THOUGHT OF YOU—A SONG.

I care not whether the skies are blue,
  Or the clouds gloom black above me;
A sweet thought comes with the thought
    of you—
  You love me, dear, you love me!

When the world is cold and its friend-
    ships few,
  And toil is a vain endeavor,
A sweet voice sings to my soul of you,
  And the world is sweet forever.

And love, my love, with the bright eyes
    true
  And the red lips kind with kisses,
There is no love like my love for you—
  No joy in the world like this is!

And whether the skies are dark or blue,
  With stars or storms above me,
My life will shine with the thought of
    you—
  You love me, dear, you love me!

KISS FOR KISS.

Just one kiss?   Nay, sweet, I know
Love would never have it so.
Should those lips of crimson stain
Kiss me, I should kiss again!
What could fairer be than this—
Love for love and kiss for kiss?

I would owe you nothing, sweet,
Not a heart's faint, fluttering beat!
When I feel your fond heart thrill,
Dearest, shall my own be still?
Nay, it must be always this—
Love for love and kiss for kiss!

Kiss for kiss; the lilies white
Kiss the wind and kiss the light;
And the wind the kiss returns,
And the light its answer burns
On the lily's lips—oh, bliss!
Love's a lily—kiss for kiss!

THE LAST INN.

This is the inn that I
  Have dreamed of all my days;
I enter—close the door—good-by!
  And the world may go its ways.
The soft, cool shadows round me creep;
I lay me down to rest—to sleep.

There is no reckoning here:
  Not any noise or strife;
Nor shall one murmur at the fare
  When Death is host to Life.
Clean bed and board for ye that come,
But sightless eyes and lips made dumb.

Cold ice at head and feet,
  But flowers of colors grand
To make the air above you sweet
  And paint the roof of sand.
What more? And when the keen winds
        blow,
Sweet dreams in daisies 'neath the snow.

Good-night, friends, and farewell!
  Our lives must parted be.
Grieve not that I with Death must dwell,
  For Death is kind to me.
Tired, I lay me down to rest,
A child lulled on a mother's breast.

MY DEAD FRIEND.

Adown the vale of Life together
We walked in spring and winter weather,
    When days were dim, when days were
       bright;
My friend of whom God's will bereft me,
Whose kind, congenial spirit left me
    And went forth in the Unknown Night.

I saw his step grow more invalid,
I saw his cheek grow pallid—pallid,
    And wither like a dying rose;
Until, at length, being all too weary
For Life's rude scenes and places dreary,
    He bade farewell to friends and foes.

This is his grave. The Spring with flowers
Bestrews it in the morning hours,
    Her rarest roses o'er him bowed;
And Summer pauses to deplore him,
And weeping Winter arches o'er him
    Her solemn drapery of cloud.

He was not faultless. God, who gave him
Life, and Christ, who died to save him,
    Sent Sorrow, wherewith he was tried;

And if, as I who loved him name him,
There should be heard a voice to blame him,
   May we not answer: "Christ hath died?"

Ah, verily! . . . I fancy often
I see his kindly features soften—
   I mark his melting eyes grow dim,
While Hunger, with its pained appealing,
Its want and woe and grief revealing,
   Stretched its imploring palms to him.

He cannot answer now.   He never,
In all the dim, vast, deep Forever,
   Shall speak with human words again.
He cannot hear the song birds calling;
He cannot feel the spring dews falling,
   Nor sigh when winter winds complain.

Deep is his sleep.   He would not waken
Though earth were to her centre shaken
   By the loud thunders of a God.
Though the strong sea, by tempest driven,
With wailing waves rock earth and heaven,
   He would not answer from the sod.

So be it, friend!   A little while hence,
And in the dear, deep, dreamless Silence
   We too shall share thy couch of rest.

When we have trod Life's pathways dreary,
Kind Death will take the hands grown
    weary,
  And gently fold them o'er the breast.

Sleep on, dear friend!   No marble column
Gleams in the lights and shadows solemn
  Over the grasses on thy grave;
But flowers bloom there—the roses love
    thee;
And the tall oaks that tower above thee
  Their broad, green banners o'er thee wave.

Sleep, while the weary years are flying;
While men are born, while men are dying!
  Sleep on thy curtained couch of sod!
Thine be the rest which Christ hath given,
Thine be the Christian's hope of Heaven;
  Thine be the perfect peace of God!

A NEW YEAR'S SONG.

O New Year! that with merry sound
   Is coming up the slope,
Pass lightly o'er that little mound
   Where lies a life's lost hope!
For you have curls of gold, New Year,
And curls of gold are resting there!

Sing, if you will, your happy stave
   O'er frosty vale and hill;
But when you pass that little grave—
   Oh, let the song be still!
For lips that knew no song of cheer
Are sleeping there—are sleeping there!

Hide not with flakes of chilly snow
   The withered flowers that rest
(Poor gifts of hearts that loved her so!)
   Upon that little breast.
The only flower two lives held dear
Lies withered at your feet, New Year!

But oh, the years must come and go,
   Nor heed our wish or will;
And yet I hope, and yet I know
   He loves His children still
Whose hand makes crosses hard to bear—
Even like this little grave, New Year!

"*NEARER TO THEE.*"

They were singing, sweetly singing,
　And the song melodiously
On the evening air was ringing:
　"Nearer, O my God, to Thee!"
In my eyes the tear-drops glistened
　As it stirred the twilight dim,
And I wondered as I listened
　If it brought them nearer Him?

Were they like the wanderer weary,
　Song and life in sweet accord;
Resting in the darkness dreary
　In that nearness to the Lord?
Had His spirit ever sought them
　To be slighted or denied?
Had that dear song ever brought them
　Closer to the Saviour's side?

I have heard its music often,
　Felt its meaning deep and sweet;
And my weary heart would soften
　Singing at my Master's feet;
"Nearer Thee,"—oh, precious feeling!—
　Nearer Thee in gain and loss;
Nearer Thee when I am kneeling
　In the shadow of Thy Cross!

Nearer Thee when Love, descending,
  Falls in blessing on my head;
Nearer Thee when I am bending
  O'er the graves that hide my dead!
Nearer Thee in joy, in sorrow,
  'Tis the same where'er I roam;
Nearer Thee to-day, to-morrow,
  O my King, my Christ, my Home!

IN THE FIELDS.

O maiden under the skies so blue,
  Of the eyes and tresses brown,
I'd rather be walking the fields with you
  Than going my way to the town!
Is it far to your dwelling? But here's a
      rose;
Perhaps you slipped from its heart—who
      knows?

It is like your face; it is like the smile
  Of your lips so red and sweet.
Do the roses bloom for a little while
  And their hearts then cease to beat?
How fair were the roses my youth-time
      knew!
Were I a rose I would bloom for you.

Do you roam through the summers sweet
  and long
 Over these fields so fair,
And blend your voice with the harvest song
 That thrills through the scented air?
When you bind the wheat with a golden
  skein
Are the tares not mixed with the ripened
  grain?

Sowing and reaping my life has known,
 And now with the gathered sheaves
There are fruitless weeds that have heedless
  grown,
 And thorns 'neath the rose's leaves.
Sowing and reaping, the harvest seems
Less than my labor and less than my dreams.

  . . . .

O maiden under the skies so blue,
 Of the eyes and tresses brown,
I'd rather be walking the fields with you
 Than going my way to the town!
Is it far to your dwelling? But here's a
  rose;
Perhaps you slipped from its heart—who
  knows?

THE CALL OF THE REAPERS.

I know that it is reaping-time in all the
    fields of Lee;
I can hear the reapers singing o'er the
    meadows, calling me:
"And wherefore come you not to-day to reap
    the golden grain?"
But I'll never see the fields of Lee, nor reap
    with them again.

"And wherefore come you not to-day?" they
    cry across the wheat;
"And wherefore come you not?" the winds
    are chiming low and sweet;
And far and near sweet sounds I hear from
    over mount and main;
But I shall not see the fields of Lee, nor
    reap in them again.

"Oh, wherefore come you not? The hand
    of autumn decks the sod;
The world is like a picture where the har-
    vests smile to God;
There's yet a late white rose for you in val-
    ley and in plain."
But I shall not see the fields of Lee, where
    blooms that rose, again.

"Ah, wherefore come you not? The doves
    have left their woodland nests,
With the gold of autumn gleaming on their
    downy, tender breasts;
And they're calling to you soft: 'Come
    home!'" But all their calls are vain;
For I shall not hear the birds sing in the
    fields of Lee again.

Oh, comrades, cease your crying, as ye reap
    in fields of Lee;
Ye have there so many reapers there is
    never need of me!
Oh, doves, leave not your nests, nor call in
    tender tones and vain,
To him who hears, with falling tears, but
    cannot come again.

Reap on, ye men and maids of Lee; for
    those that sow must reap;
And I am reaping far away, while ye your
    vigils keep;
But there is no song upon my lips, nor golden
    is the grain,
And I shall not see the fields of Lee, nor
    reap with you again!

SLAIN.

Swiftly the shot from my rifle sped
To his heart, and he fell in the darkness—
    dead!

With never a struggle, never a sigh,
I saw my enemy bleed and die.

And now, I said, is my peace secure;
I shall fear his hand and his hate no more.

The black night came with a stealthy pace
And shed the shadows over his face,

Hidden forever from mortal view:
And only God and the darkness knew!

But what would I barter of good and fair
To take the place of the dead man there,

As I face the future—the life to be,
With God and the darkness haunting me!

IN A SWING.

Here's a picture of the spring
      (Happy spring!) —
It is beauty in a swing
      (Such a swing!)
Made of vines from garden bowers
Where the blossoms fall in showers,
With embroidery of flowers—
      Pretty thing!

She is Beauty.   Up she goes
      In the air,
And there tumbles down a rose
      From her hair.
I can catch—I will not miss it—
Tumble, tumble—ah, this is it,
And with lips of love I kiss it
      For my dear.

"Swing me! swing me!"   It is clear
      I am caught
In a fairy, silken snare,
      All for naught;
For her sweet commands are ringing
And she will not cease the swinging,
Though the birds of love are singing—
      Happy lot!

"Swing me, swing me!" How her tones
    Ring and ring,
Till the heart within me groans—
    Tired thing!
But her heart is like a feather;
Would to heaven in just such weather
We could go through life together
    In a swing!

FOR YOU.

For you, dear heart, the light—
    God's smile, where'er you be,
And if He will—the night,
    Only the night for me!

For you Love's own dear land
    Of roses, fair and free;
And if you will—no hand
    To give a rose to me.

For you Love's dearest bliss
    In all the years to be;
And if you will—no kiss
    Of any love for me.

Thankful to know you blest,
    When God your brow adorns
With the sweet roses of His rest,
    I thank Him for the thorns!

LOVE'S VISITOR.

I see her in the near light, in the far light,
  In the morning, when the sunbeams kiss
    the dew;
In the evening, when the shimmer of the
    starlight
  The tangle of the vines comes peeping
    through;

And her eyes, as in the sweet and far-away
    time,
  Are beautiful and tender; and her cheek
Is fragrant with the freshness of the May
    time—
  But the rosy lips are silent when I speak!

Perhaps the loving name by which I knew
    her
  Is not the name by which they know her
    there
Beyond—where stars are brighter, skies are
    bluer,
  Where never any darkness draweth near.

Perhaps the woven love words that I bring
    her
  She treasures in sweet silence, little worth:

She'd rather hear the songs the angels sing
  her,
Than listen to the lowlier songs of earth.

Yet wherefore from the seraph-guarded
  portal
Beyond, where flows the dark, dividing
  sea,
Whose waters lave the shining shore im-
  mortal,
In light and night comes back my love to
  me?

Forever comes?   Oh, doubting heart! no
  Heaven—
Howe'er its walls may tower the stars
  above,
With gates that look down on the unfor-
  given,
Can stay the hands that love holds out to
  love!

STANLEY'S MESSAGE.

How did the men with Stanley die?
Under the blazing Afric sky,

Struck by the python's fangs, or slain
By poisoned arrows that fell like rain;

Or tracked and torn on the desert way
By hungry lions that watch for prey.

The desert's sands and the Congo's flood
Were crimsoned deep with their sacred blood.

Brave and faithful they were; but one—
Though his life is ended, his mission done,

Lives in the love of our hearts again—
Best and bravest of Stanley's men!

For lo! when the black king—savage, grim,
Stayed the leader and heard from him

How One called Christ on the cross had died,
Scourged and bleeding and crucified,

He cried: "O brother! across the sea
Send this Christ of the cross to me!"

Then Stanley summoned his men and said:
"The way ye have travelled is reeking red

With the blood of your hearts. But who
     will bear
This message? Ho! for a volunteer!"

Then out from the ranks came one and said:
"Be mine the duty," and bowed his head.

Then Stanley traced with a trembling hand
These words: "Send Christ to this darkened
     land!"

II.

Over the desert scorched and bare;
Swift through the forest wild and drear;

Leaping light by the lion's lair;
Coiled sleek serpents that hissed in air;

By the unseen foe that hurled the dart
Or winged the arrow after his heart,

Sped a brave and bleeding man
To Gordon's camp in the far Soudan.

And the goal is gained, and they crowd
     around
A bleeding form on the holy ground,

(Made holy then!) and they strive to wrest
The poisoned shaft from his crimson breast.

No word he said as his glazing eyes
Looked their last on the world and skies;

But the brave hand pointed the bloody way
To the heart where the letter of Stanley lay,

Rent by the fierce and fatal dart
And stained by the blood of his faithful
          heart!

Only these words, in Stanley's hand:
"Send the Christ to this darkened land!"

.   .   .   .

Was this the message of high emprise?
Ay!   And down from the Christ's own skies

Swiftly the sorrowing angels came,
With wings of white and swords of flame—

Came, in the arms of love to take
The life that died for the dear Christ's sake;

The life whose record was written then:
"Best and bravest of Stanley's men!"

THE VIOLET.

In life's last, lone December
  There blooms one violet.
But why should I remember
  When she can so forget?
She will not mourn or miss it
  When cruel frosts shall kill;
But lean, fond lips, and kiss it,
  For we remember still!

In unknown paths and places
  Her fairy steps may be,
But still her pictured face is
  The dearest dream to me;
And though the skies above me
  With stormy scenes are set,
The dark eyes seem to love me—
  Ah, how could they forget?

Oh, that the winds might waft her
  This dying violet's breath;
That I might follow after
  And die the violet's death!
For then her heart, believing,
  Would leave, poor, wounded dove,
Upon my lips, half grieving,
  The first, last kiss of love!

NO CROSS, NO CROWN.

I sometimes think, when life seems drear
And gloom and darkness gather here;
When Hope's bright star forsakes my skies
And sorrow o'er my pathway lies,
It would be sweet, it would be best
To fold my tired hands and rest;
But then God sends an angel down
Who sweetly says: "No Cross, no Crown."

I heard the reckless river moan
With sad and melancholy tone;
I saw its waters flashing free
And dashing to the distant sea.
I would have plunged beneath its tide
And on its friendly bosom died,
But then God sent the angel down
Who whispered sweet: "No Cross, no
    Crown."

Then turned I from the river's shore
To bear my bitter task once more;
With aching heart and burning head
To battle for my crust of bread.
But Hunger came, who knew me well,
And fainting by the way I fell;
But still the angel fluttered down,
And weeping said: "No Cross, no Crown."

No Cross, no Crown! While standing there
The cross too heavy seemed to bear,
And for the crown—I could not see
That it was ever meant for me!
The words I could not understand
E'en while I pressed the angel's hand;
But still he looked with pity down,
And still he said: "No Cross, no Crown."

I said: "The world is dark and lone;
There is no hand to hold my own:
I cannot bear the noonday heat,
The sharp thorns pierce my bleeding feet!"
"Behold," he cried, "where, sacrificed,
Shine the red, bleeding wounds of Christ!"
And fell his tears of mercy down
While still he said: "No Cross, no Crown."

Back to the world I turned again
To court life's joys, endure its pain,
But all the sweetness that it gave
I followed weeping to the grave;
And from the cold and quiet sod
I raised my streaming eyes to God,
And saw the angel coming down
And in his hands a golden crown!

Then did I laugh at earthly loss,
And, kneeling, lifted up the cross,
Though all that once made life so sweet
Lay 'neath the lilies at my feet.

A radiance from the realms of light
Flashed for a moment on my sight;
A still, small voice came fluttering down:
"It is enough. Receive the crown!"

SAINT SIMON'S SOUND.

How mad the white stars danced that night—
　　A wild and merry round,
As fast we fled in foam and light
　　Across Saint Simon's Sound.

The sail, like some glad gull's white wing,
　　Still made the vessel bound
And speed, as if a living thing,
　　Across Saint Simon's Sound.

I did not heed the lamps that flashed
　　From warning towers around,
As through the dark and light we dashed
　　Across Saint Simon's Sound.

I did not fear the roaring sea
　　Where love is whelmed and drowned—
Your gold hair blowing over me
　　On sweet Saint Simon's Sound.

Your soft white arms about my neck—
    A splendid necklace wound,
White as the foam that washed the deck
    On glad Saint Simon's Sound.

Mine was no heart to faint or fear
    When roared the storm profound;
I only knew that Love was near
    On sweet Saint Simon's Sound.

I only felt his living breath,
    And for that rapture found,
I dared the danger and the death
    Across Saint Simon's Sound.

When lightning quivered from the skies,
    In stormy darkness drowned,
Fair flashed the starlight from your eyes
    On dark Saint Simon's Sound.

That starlight which with beams divine
    Made bright the world around,
Till God's own glory seemed to shine
    Above Saint Simon's Sound.

Oh, dark and light and storm and night,
    And waves where love is drowned,
Give back to me that dream so bright
    On sweet Saint Simon's Sound!

And take these rainbows arching peace
  In skies by sunlight crowned,
For love, in storms that never cease
  On dark Saint Simon's Sound!

LOVE'S BOUQUET.

Red roses, wherefrom the dew drips,
  Staining the turf at my feet,
You were never as red as her lips—
  Or as sweet!

Blue violets, tender and true—
  A mirror for sun-sprinkled skies,
Do you think you were ever as blue
  As her eyes?

Rare lilies, in garments of white,
  Which winds with warm kisses beguile,
Have you yet known a sunbeam as bright
  As her smile?

Kiss, lily, rose, violet—kiss!
  Ere time doth your beauty destroy;
For her white hand hath touched you, and
    this
  Is your joy!

THROUGH THE WHEAT.

When she came tripping through the wheat
It seemed to bend to kiss her feet,
And roses all the sod made sweet
    And birds sang cheery;

The honey-bees were humming low—
Gold specks on roses white as snow,
Sweet roses—not so sweet, I know,
    As she was—Mary!

Her footstep seemed to wake a sound
Of tinkling music from the ground
That thrilled the winds that whistled round
    With sweet caresses,

And on her forehead, white and sleek,
The rarest blossoms fell to wreak
Their love, and played at hide-and-seek
    In her gold tresses.

Down fell the scythe upon the grass,
And "Mary, Mary, will you pass?"
"You're in my way," she said. "Alas!
    I must be going!"

"Not till you pay the forfeit sweet
Of coming this way through the wheat;
Ah! Mary—lips were made to meet—
    A kiss you're owing!"

Up went the dainty finger-tips,
To shield the rich and rosy lips,
And all their red was in eclipse—
    My luck seemed missing.

A moment only! Then, as she
Fled like a shaft of light from me,
She cried: "I paid no forfeit—see?
    You did the kissing!"

THE AFTER-TIME.

There cometh a time for laughter,
    And joy for the days and years;
But ever there cometh after
    A time and a place for tears.
We weary of revel and riot,
    And sick of the worldly strife;
God sendeth the peace, the quiet,
    That quicken the founts of life.

And the spirit is disenchanted
    With joys that are bitter-sweet;
And the soul which for rest hath panted
    Falls down at the Master's feet;

The world and its ways seem lonely
    And love at the best seems loss—
What help is there then but only
    To cling to the crimson cross?

To cling to the cross that blossoms
    With blood for the erring shed,
On the tenderest of tender bosoms
    To pillow the weary head,
To feel the love that is glowing
    From the heart that is quick to beat,
With even the harsh nails going
    In the beautiful scarred white feet!

O bird by the storm-winds driven
    Where never a sweet bird sings,
From the wild and angry heaven
    Fly homeward with weary wings!
And ye that are worn and weary—
    Who faint by the way and fall,
Fly fast from the darkness dreary
    To the Rock that was cleft for all!

LOVE'S THANKSGIVING.

Thanksgiving for you, dear—a sweet thanks-
   giving
For what you were in all the past to me;
For what you are—a joy that sweetens
   living—
For what you are to be.

Thanksgiving for those eyes—the kind, the
   splendid—
   Dear eyes, whose light the whole wide world
      would miss;
Your voice, in which all melodies are
   blended—
   Thanksgiving for your kiss!

Thanksgiving for your smile, like sunlight
   streaming
   Over my heart, which still for you must
      beat;
Dear, if to love you be but idle dreaming,
   Never was dream so sweet!

Thanksgiving for you! Though my heart
   shall miss you,
   Drifting like some wrecked vessel far at
      sea;
I lean toward you in the dark and kiss you—
   Sweetheart, kiss me!

HUNT HIM DOWN.

Ho! good people of every town,
Here is a brother: hunt him down!
Roar at his heels like a raging flood—
Slake your thirst with his heart's red blood;
For he was tempted—he sinned, he fell
From heights of heaven to depths of hell!
Fugitive—fleeing the saintly town,
Hunt him down! Hunt him down!

Ho! good people of every town,
Sage and sinner and knave and clown,
Swell the ranks with their storm and strife
In the maddening race for a human life!
Pause not ye for his gasp and groan—
Aim the arrow and hurl the stone!
Past the village and through the town
Hunt him down! Hunt him down!

Care not ye for the grief he feels;
Let the bloodhounds howl at his burning
          heels;
Let the cold, sharp stones of the cruel street
Pierce the wounds in his bleeding feet!
Hurl your hisses and block his way,
Till he stands at last like a beast at bay!
Search the village and sack the town—
Hunt him down! Hunt him down!

Ho! good people of every town,
Let not mercy your justice drown;
'Tis human game—'tis a soul in woe,
Whose white Redeemer died long ago!
Scourge him—slay him! 'tis little loss:
A sinner clings to the crimson cross,
Asking not for your shining crown,
Dead in the darkness—hunted down!

GOING HOME.

Adieu, sweet friends; I have waited long
  To hear the message that calls me home,
And now it comes like a low, sweet song
  Of welcome over the river's foam.
And my heart shall ache, and my feet shall
    roam
No more—no more! I am going home.

I am going home. O'er the river's tide,
  Crystal-white in the noonday sun,
I see the friends on the other side
  Who the beautiful pearly gates have won;
And far and sweet from the shining dome
They call to me still—come home! come
    home!

Do not weep for me, friends; but lay
  Peacefully over my silent breast
The hands whose labor is done, and say:
  "He hath entered in at the gates of rest."
And God is merciful—God knows best,
And sweet to the weary is rest, sweet rest!

Why should I linger? I long to go,
  And though "no price in my hand I
    bring,"
The Christ who died for us loves us so!
  And simply still to His cross I cling.
Never more from that cross to roam,
I am going home! I am going home!

Home! where no storm and no tempest
    raves
  In the light of the calm, eternal day;
Where no willows droop over lonely graves
  And tears from our eyes shall be wiped
    away.
And my heart shall ache and my feet shall
    roam
No more—no more! I am going home.

THE NEW LOVE AND THE OLD.

Gone is the old-time glory—the passion and
  pain of love,
When the world heard the wondrous story
  and smiled to the skies above;
When the rivers rippled and glistened, and
  music thrilled from the birds,
And the roses blushed as they listened, and
  the winds and the waves had words.

Gone are the dreams, the fancies and fears
  that once were Love's;
Stolen kisses and tender glances, seen only
  by mating doves
In the paths where the fairies led us—the
  beautiful paths and sweet,
Where Love his litany read us in the violets
  at our feet.

Memories, these! Do we miss them — the
  wonderful days of old?
Would we cherish them, keep them, kiss
  them, as misers cherish their gold?
Ah, dear, had those days the sweetness of
  the latter, lovelier days
When love in its all-completeness is blossom-
  ing 'round our ways?

No dreams—for the world is real—torture
    and tempt me now;
You are my soul's ideal, my queen of the
    crownless brow!
Then I was mad with the meaning a look or
    a tone expressed;
Then you were shyly leaning away from my
    waiting breast.

But now, with your white arms twining—a
    necklace—around me, I
Can see in your bright eyes' shining a love
    that can never die;
The love that the years have hastened; that
    will live in the years to be;
Tender and true and chastened, and dearer
    than life to me!

And, sweet, if we loved each other in the
    beautiful blossomed past,
Still clinging to one another, we who loved
    first, love last!
But the last love is the best love—and only
    the sweeter grows:
You were then a bud on my breast, love,
    but now you're a full-blown rose!

HER BEAUTIFUL HANDS.

God's roses are sweet and His lilies are fair
  As they bend 'neath the dews from above;
They are splendid and fair—but they can-
        not compare
  With the beautiful hands of my love.
No jewels adorn them—no glittering bands—
They are just as God made them, these
        sweet, sweet hands!

And not for earth's gems, or its bright dia-
        dems,
  Or the pearls from the depths of the sea,
Or the queens of the lands with their beauti-
        ful hands
  Should these dear hands be taken from me.
What exquisite blisses await their com-
        mands!
They were made for my kisses, these dear,
        sweet hands.

Ay, made for my kisses! And when, some
        day,
  My life shall be robbed of its trust,
And the lips that are colder shall kiss them
        away
  And hide them in daisies and dust;

I will kneel in the dark where the angel
    stands,
And my kiss shall be last on these dear, sweet
    hands.

LITTLE HANDS.

Little hands whose work is o'er;
Tired hands that toil no more;
Tender little hands that rest
Folded o'er the sinless breast—
Bending o'er them mother stands,
Kisses still these little hands.

God, who ever does the best,
Folded them and bade them rest.
Would He then these hands condemn
With a mother's kiss on them
When they reach the shining lands?
Mother loved these little hands!

Mother loved them in the past,
Mother's kiss was on them last;
Little hands, beneath the sod,
Take a mother's kiss to God!
Waft it o'er the shining sands,
Little snow-white angel hands.

WRITING FOR BREAD.

I sit alone—alone to-night,
A shadow in the ghastly light
That feebly flickers, faintly falls
On cold, damp floor and barren walls;
And o'er a desk of structure rude
I bend in melancholy mood:
For whether grief distract my breast,
Or rob my weary eyes of rest,
It matters not: by Hunger led,
I still must write, must write for bread!

I sit alone; but is it strange?
Through toil and sorrow, chance and
    change,
I have sat thus for many years,
In pain, in poverty and tears;
Until my rapid, restless pen
Has glided, o'er and o'er again,
Into my heart, crushed by despair,
As if to steal the life-blood there!
But what is heart, and what is head
To him who writes, and writes for bread?

The world to me is like a dream:
Once—once I saw its beauties beam,

In the sad, perished long ago,
Before my life was blighted so.
I loved my brothers, all that earth
Contained of tenderness and worth;
I held their love a shining gem,
And sang my sweetest songs to them;
But banished from their breasts I fled,
And here, alone, I write for bread.

Ah, God, what misery is mine!
These stars, these cold, calm stars of Thine
That gem the silent midnight skies
Are not as sleepless as my eyes!
They—they have seen my life-blood drip,
For we have held companionship;
And I have read them o'er in vain,
Until they burned into my brain.
I mark the scornful rays they shed
On him who writes, and writes for bread.

Cold, cruel lamp, thy spectral ray
Shall flicker like my life away:
For by this heart by sorrow crushed,
And by this brow with madness flushed,
This hollow check and sunken eye,
These lips, too feeble for a sigh,
I feel that life, even in its noon,
Is ebbing and will vanish soon.
Then, weary heart and aching head,
We shall not need to write for bread!

Then will they lay me down to rest,
And gently fold across my breast
The hands whose weary work is o'er,
And close the eyes that weep no more.
And they will take from my cold clasp
The pen that felt my living grasp,
And calm and sweet my rest shall be,
Though not an eye will weep for me.
The dust will be a sweeter bed
To him who, dying, wrote for bread.

HER VALENTINE.

What shall I send you for a valentine?
  Perhaps there is nothing that would please
    me better
Than to enclose this loving heart of mine
  Within the snowy pages of my letter.
That would be very innocent and artless;
But, then, I know that you would deem me
  heartless.

But take it, love, such as it is—a true
  And trusting heart. You did not seek to
    win it;
Unconsciously the poor thing went to you,
  Dreaming, and dazzled in one golden
    minute!
Let it be thrall to you; (sweet service this is!)
Its only recompense your smiles and kisses!

A MEMORY.

I sit alone in my room to-night
    And think of her dear, sweet face—
Here where I miss the tender light
    Of her loveliness and grace.

I read her letters over again—
    The letters she wrote last year;
The faded flowers in the folds remain
    As her white hands placed them there.

Ah, little she thought when these flowers
        she pressed
    For the heart that adored her so,
They'd soon be blooming above her breast,
    And she in the dust below!

But the beat of her holy heart was stilled
    Ere the voice in its depths could speak,
And the Angel of Death, in his anger, chilled
    The rose of life on her cheek.

Why do I read her letters o'er?
    Can they bring her back as of old?
The hand that penned them can write no
        more,
    The lips that kissed them are cold!

Dear heart, we shall meet when the years
 are past,
 Under the dawn and dew,
And light will break on my life at last
 When I dream in the dust with you!

IF YOU COULD COME.

If you could come to me as I recall
 Your face, and I could feel upon my brow
 The warm breath of those lips, so silent
  now—
Could hear some word from them in music
 fall,
Thrilling the silence in my life with all
 The old-time sweetness! If I could but
  hear,
When the sun sinks behind the western wall
 And twilight shades the weeping atmos-
  phere,
 A rustle in the roses at the gate,
And, looking, I should see you standing
  there—
 My lonely life would not be desolate,
For this would comfort all my soul's
  despair.
I know thy life is lovelier—God knows best,
But still the dove mourns o'er its empty nest.

A SONG OF BLESSING.

God's blessing, gentle eyes,
Upon you for the glance you gave to-day;
   Low 'neath your light my heart your
      debtor lies,
Striving to find some thankful words to say.

God's blessing, gentle lips,
Upon you for a tender smile—like this!
   His reddest rose with loveliest crimson tips
Your parted petals, quivering with a kiss.

God's blessing, gentle hand,
Upon your downy whiteness, and the touch
   That thrills me so! I cannot understand—
Hands, lips, and eyes, I love you all so much!

God's blessing for you, dear;
For all you are, and all that you may be;
   Your glance, your kiss, your smile, your
      touch—the mere
Thought of you! Ah, how dear you are to
      me!

ONE SAD DAY.

One sad day when the sun's gold crown
    Jewelled the desolate, dreamy west,
I came with a burden, and laid it down
    Under the lilies and leaves to rest;
And, weeping, I left it and went my way
    With the Twilight whispering: "God
      knows best!"

One sweet day—it was long ago,
    And thorny the paths my feet have pressed
Since with tears and kisses I laid it low—
    Soul of my soul and life of my breast!
But kneeling now in the dark to pray,
    There comes with a song from the sunless
      west
The same sweet voice that I heard that day—
    The Twilight whispering: "God knows
      best!"

RESOLUTION.

Poor? Yea, I grant it! In the lowliest
    ways
My feet shall tread until they gain the goal;
But not too poor—thank God!—to make my
    days
    Rich with the deeds that glorify the soul.

Thorns? Yea! they pierce me; but I will not
    bow
Till every thorn hath for a sin sufficed;
I wear them for a crown upon my brow—
    Sweet with the memory of a dying Christ.

Upward and onward still shall press my feet,
    No cross shall daunt me, though no crown
    I win;
Faithful, unswerving, till I hear the sweet
    "Well done" of Him whose servant I have
    been.

AFTER DEATH.

All night long the dead man lay
Under the leaves and rain-washed clay;

All night long in her dwelling dim
The wife of his bosom wept for him.

" And my heart is buried with him," she said,
" For I loved him living—I love him dead!"

And the dead man dreamed in his narrow
      place
That he felt her tears fall over his face;

And no dreams of the dead could sweeter be—
"Down to death she was true to me!"

But when o'er his grave, in the shine and rain,
Roses withered and bloomed again;

When the leaves fell brown on the cold
      earth's crust,
And his bones were white and his heart was
      dust;

The woman he loved to another said:
"I love you more than I loved the dead!"

And in that same hour the only rose
That bloomed on a grave fell dead!   .   .   .
   Who knows

If the dead can feel?   But howe'er it be,
Sweet, with the love that you have for me,

Love me now, while I draw my breath;
Love me down to the gates of death!

This is all that I ask or crave—
Love thrives ill on a voiceless grave!

THY FACE.

Thy face is with me when I walk alone
  In thorny ways of sorrow and of night;
  Thy smile my comfort and thine eyes my
    light,
Lest I should dash my foot against a stone.
And oft the tender thought of thee, my own,
  Sustains me when I waver and grow weak.
Tempted, I call to mind thy farewell tone—
  The kiss I left upon thy conscious cheek
At parting—and I feel thy presence near,
A joy to comfort and a strength to bear!
  O dear, sweet face, be near me all the while;
O eyes of light, dispel the darkness drear;
  O lips, beam on me with a loving smile,
And I the wreath of victory shall wear!

FAITHFUL.

It is something, sweet, when the world goes
　　ill
To know you are faithful and love me still;
To see, when the sunshine has left the skies,
The love-light shining in your dear eyes;
Beautiful eyes, more dear to me
Than all the wealth of the world could be!

It is something, dearest, to feel you near
When life with its sorrows seems hard to
　　bear;
To feel when I falter the clasp divine
Of your tender and trusting hand in mine;
Beautiful hand, more dear to me
Than the tenderest things of earth could be!

Sometimes, dearest, the world goes wrong,
For God gives grief with His gift of song,
And poverty, too!　But your love is more
To me than riches and golden store;
Beautiful love, until death shall part
It is mine, as you are—my own sweetheart!

ONE OF THE KING'S OWN GIRLS.

So fair and fleet are her dancing feet
    In the music's waves and whirls,
My heart keeps time with a rhythmic beat—
    She is one of the king's own girls!

The king is great in his robes of state—
    In his purple robes and white,
And I crouch low down at his palace gate—
    Where her white feet flash to-night.

And I kiss a rose, and its warm breath goes
    Through the portals, wild and sweet:
And it sighs and dies 'neath her splendid eyes,
    In the flash of her fairy feet.

It sighs and dies like the heart that lies
    In the warmth of her winsome breath;
For I kissed her lips and I kissed her eyes
    With my soul, and to kiss means death!

But so fair and fleet were her dancing feet
    In the music's waves and whirls,
My heart died gladly with one wild beat
    For one of the king's own girls!

WAY-WORN.

I say to my soul that it would be best
  If the hands that labor were folded o'er
The silent breast in the last sweet rest—
    When I think of the friends who have
      gone before,
Who have crossed o'er the river's rolling
    tide
And reached the home on the other side.

It seems so far to the wished-for day,
  And weary and lonely and lost I roam;
I feel like a child who has lost his way
    And is always longing for home, sweet
      home;
But I say to my yearning heart—"Be still:
We'll go home when it is God's will."

The night is long, but the day will break
    When the light of eternity, streaming
      down
On the cross we bear for the Master's sake,
    Will guide our steps to the promised crown.
A little while and the gate is passed—
Home and heaven and rest at last!

THE VALES OF ROME.

No cold and crumbling arches—
    The frolic of the Fates;
No senatorial marches
    Through lion-guarded gates;
No Cæsar's glittering legions,
    Whose eagles crown its dome;
But love, in Love's own regions—
    The violet-vales of Rome.

There rise the dark-blue mountains,
    Where clouds are fair and fleet;
There leap the living fountains—
    There sing the rivers sweet!
There morning breaks in showers
    Of light and silver foam,
And from their airy towers
    Smile stormless stars on Rome.

And there rare birds are winging
    Their wild and wondrous flight;
The splendid day dies singing
    A love song to the night;
And Love's sweet voices calling
    Love's weary wanderers home,
In golden music falling,
    Thrill all the vales of Rome.

That Love which woos and wonders
  Far from the wreck and strife,
I hear it in the thunders
  And tempests of my life;
And answer: "Love, I hear thee,
  O'er seas of storm and foam;
Thy lover's steps draw near thee—
  Ring sweet, ye bells of Rome!"

LOVE'S RETROSPECT.

We sat there yester even beneath the listen-
    ing vines,
Where still the mornin' glory above the
    doorway twines,
And the nightingales were singin' just as
    they sang of yore,
When first she said "I love you," but now
    she loves me more!

The same old place; the rocker in which she
    sat while I,
Half fearful that the stars would hear the
    secret in the sky,
Leaned her way just a little, and said, "I
    love you!" Sure,
I meant it then, and loved her true, but now
    I love her more!

The old days seemed to come again while
    sitting side by side
Where first she said she'd be my wife—we
    didn't call it "bride"—
I told her then, "How sweet you are!" an'
    felt my pulses thrill
With all that sweetness close to me—but
    now she's sweeter still!

We talked it over, sitting there, near love's
    own happy lands,
And once more felt the first sweet joy that
    comes of holdin' hands;
She seemed to be my sweetheart still—'twas
    all just as before—
But we clasped each other closer, and we
    loved each other more!

A CHRISTMAS COMEDY.

Two shrouded shapes on Christmas Eve,
  Grim, ghostly, met
Where winds in weird numbers grieve
  And raindrops wet

The leaky roofs where dead men dream
  With stifled moans;
The chill white starlight's dagger-gleam
  Laid bare their bones.

"Away," cried one, "from death and dark—
  Where dead men be,
To where the world is blazing.   Hark!
  Its revelry!"

Then through the dreary night they sped,
  With wild desires,
Where life with love and laughter fed
  The Christmas fires.

When lo! one standing near a hearth
  Where love did dwell,
Heard a child's wailing at its birth,
  And shuddering fell;

His white bones strewn about the place,
 His sockets dull,
Light's mockery! And before Love's face
 His staring skull!

The other, warming at the blaze,
 By Love's own side,
Dreaming of life and of the days,
 Love glorified,

Caught in his frozen bones the heat
 Life only knew;
The red flames thawed the graveyard sleet
 And pierced him through.

Then creaked his bones, and one by one
 They crumbled white;
His skull stared as his friend's had done
 And blurred the light.

And when I left—too sad to say,
 But so it comes—
Full fifty children were at play,
 With skulls for drums!

A CHRISTMAS HYMN.*

From the centuries far away,
On the kneeling world to-day
Shines one splendid star—the gem
Of the stars of Bethlehem.

(O Christ, for whom its beams were shed,
Lo! we were to Thy manger led
With those that loved Thee, knelt with
    them!
Remember us at Bethlehem!)

It is shining as when sweet,
While their flocks fed at their feet,
Dreamed the shepherds, and its beams
Made the glory in their dreams.

(O Christ, the gentle and the sweet,
We kiss Thy hands, we kiss Thy feet!
Though all our sins our love condemn,
Do thou remember Bethlehem!)

---

* The above poem appeared as the leading Christmas
editorial in the Atlanta *Constitution*, December 25, 1891.

Ring, ye bells, your welcome! Hail,
Through the morning's misty veil,
Love's own priceless diadem
On the brow of Bethlehem!

(O Christ, Thy dreaming face at rest
Upon the blessed Mother's breast;
Let not Thy lips our kiss condemn—
Dream of us now at Bethlehem!)

Ring, ye bells! the stars above
Tell the story, sweet with love;
Ring the glory that it gives—
How Love dies, and dying lives!

(O Christ, the merciful and sweet,
For those sharp nails that pierced Thy feet;
Thy crown of thorns, our crown to be,
Remember us at Calvary!)

Sing, ye herald angels, sing,
While the bells the music ring,
Sing the message once again:
"Peace on earth, good-will to men!"

(O Christ, the crowned and glorified,
Teach us Thy love—the love that died
And lives—and for Thy sacrifice
Remember us in Paradise!)

MAID O' THE MIST.

Are you watching the ships sailing south-
    ward,
  O mystical Maid o' the Mist?
Do you wave your white hand
When they're nearing the land—
  Are the tips of your white fingers kissed
To the captains and sailors who shout o'er
    the foam
For joy of the lights in the harbor at home?

Are you watching the ships sailing south-
    ward,
  O beautiful Maid o' the Mist?
When the waves on the bars
Make their moan to the stars,
  Do you keep with the night winds a tryst?
The watch-fires are dead on the desolate
    strand
And darkness hath hidden thy beckoning
    hand.

You are watching the ships sailing south-
        ward,
  O Maid o' the Mist! but I know
That the pitiful waves
Never tell of the graves
  Fathoms and fathoms below;
And the winds that blow inland o'er sea and
        o'er sound
In mercy have stifled the cries of the
        drowned!

SONGS OF THE SOIL.

SONGS OF THE SOIL.

THE LOVE FEAST AT WAYCROSS.

It was in the town o' Waycross, not many
    weeks ago.
They had a big revival thar, as like enough
    you know;
An' though many was converted an' for par-
    don made to call,
Yet the Sunday mornin' love feast was the
    happiest time of all!

'Twas a great experience meetin', an' it done
    me good to hear
The brotherin an' the sisterin that talked re-
    ligion there;
You didn't have to ax them, nor coax them
    with a song,
Them people had religion, an' they told it
    right along!

6

Thar was one—a hard old sinner—'pears like
    I knowed his name,
But I reckon I've forgot it—who to the altar
    came;
An' he took the leader by the hand, with
    beamin' face an' bright,
An' said: "I'm comin' home, dear fren's;
    I'm comin' home to-night!"

Then a woman rose an' axed to be remem-
    bered in their prayers:
"My husband's comin' home," said she,
    a-sheddin' thankful tears;
"I want you all to pray for him; he's lived
    in sin's control,
But I think the love o' Jesus is a-breakin' on
    his soul!"

Then a young man rose an' told 'em he had
    wandered far away,
But felt like comin' home ag'in, an' axed
    'em all to pray;
An' sich a pra'r they made for him! I'll
    hear the like no more
Till I hear the sweeter music on the bright
    celestial shore.

Any shoutin'? Well, I reckon so! One
    brother give a shout:
Said he had so much religion he was 'bliged
    to let it out!
An' the preacher joined the chorus, sayin':
    "Brotherin, let 'er roll!
A man can't keep from shoutin' with relig-
    ion in his soul!"

I tell you, 'twas a happy time; I wished
    'twould never end:
Each sinner in the church that day had Je-
    sus for a friend;
But a good old deacon said to 'em, while
    tears stood in his eye:
"Thar's a better time than this, dear fren's,
    a-comin' by an' by!"

I hope some day those brotherin'll meet with
    one accord
In the higher, holier love feast, whose leader
    is the Lord;
An' when this life is over, with its sorrow an'
    its sighs,
May the little church at Waycross join the
    great church in the skies!

TO ROBERT J. BURDETTE.

I've bin readin' of your writin's, Bob, for
    many a year gone by;
They're jes like household words ter me, an'
    mixed with wet an' dry;
But of all things you've written, I think the
    sweetest still
Is them lines erbout Jim Riley and that
    night at Shelbyville!

I ain't so tender-hearted as a feller might
    suppose,
Though I wouldn't press a thorn agenst the
    white breast of a rose;
But readin' o' that piece o' your'n I felt the
    warm tears fill
My eyes—as ef I'd bin thar, in that room at
    Shelbyville.

We know Jim Riley down this way—I think
    you call him "Jim"— .
An' we'd enjoy a settin' up in any place with
    him;
He's got the run o' all our hearts—we love
    him well; but yet
Thar's a powerful sight o' feelin' 'mong us
    all fer Bob Burdette!

You seem ter think, like Riley did, you're
    "no account at all,"
But thar's not a rose you planted but has
    climbed above the wall
An' spilled its fragrance on us! You're "the
    best one of 'em yet!"
An' our hearts can hold Jim Riley without
    crowdin' Bob Burdette.

Though the "Sweet, old-fashioned Roses" in
    the old-time ways may grow,
Yet "The Gray Day" has its flowers, sleepin'
    somewhere 'neath the snow;
An' "Mists are kissed from laughin' skies"
    that shine serenely yet—
An' ef Jim's "the same old Riley," you're
    the same old Bob Burdette.

I'm runnin' on confusely; but I keep er
    thinkin' still
Of what you told us 'bout that night you
    spent at Shelbyville;
An' ef you ever steer this way, I hope you'll
    not forget
That when it comes ter "settin' up," we're
    with you, Bob Burdette!

SUMMER-TIME IN GEORGIA.

O summer-time in Georgy, I love to sing
    your praise,
When the green is on the melon an' the sun
    is on the blaze;
When the birds are pantin', chantin', an'
    jes' rantin' round the rills
With the juice of ripe blackberries jes'
    a-drippin' from their bills!

Oh summer-time in Georgy, when through
    leaves of green an' brown
The bright an' violet-scented dews jes' rain
    their richness down
On the cool an' clingin' grasses where the
    fickle sunbeam slips,
An' the famished lily puckers up its white
    resplendent lips!

O summer-time in Georgy, with the glory
    in the dells,
Where the rare an' rainy incense from the
    fresh'nin' shower swells,

An' o'er the bars to twinklin' stars float
    twilight's sad farewells
In the lowin' of the cattle an' the tinklin' o'
    the bells!

O summer-time in Georgy, when 'neath the
    listenin' vine,
Where the purple mornin' glory an' the
    honey-suckle twine,
The whippoorwills were singin' their notes
    o' love and bliss,
An' to my lips were clingin' the lips I used
    to kiss.

Stay, like a dream eternal, while dearest
    dreams depart,
An' rain your honey sweetness in showers
    round my heart.
Pshaw! I'm gettin' so pathetic my eyes can
    hardly see:
O summer-time in Georgy! You're the best
    o' times to me.

THE PICNIC AT SELINA.

That picnic at Selina—it covered lots o'
    ground;
Thar was wimmen, men an' hosses from fifty
    miles around,
An' fiddles squeaked an' brogans creaked
    the merriest kind o' song,
An' 'twas "Balance to your partners!" an'
    "Swing!" the whole day long.

'Twas a powerful site o' pleasure jes' to see
    the fellers whirl
Them lovely forms in calico, an' swing girl
    after girl.
It was quite intoxicatin'; you could hear
    the rafters ring
Till the old men couldn't stand it, an' cut
    the "pigeon-wing!"

The old-time "double-shuffle" made the dust
    fly from their heels,
An' 'twas sich a jolly scuffle in the Old Vir-
    ginny reels;

The young men jes' a-sweatin', an' the rosy
　　gals a-blowin'—
But they didn't mind the weather while they
　　kept the fiddle goin'!

"It's jolly!" roared the rafters. "It's pain-
　　ful!" groaned the floor.
"It's dusty!" said the wimmen, but they
　　only danced the more.
An' the young men called it "stavin," an'
　　I think that they was right,
For the old-time Georgia "breakdown" made
　　the stars dance with delight!

All day the fiddle's music was ringin' wild
　　an' sweet,
The nigger-parson rolled it off an' kept
　　time with his feet;
All day, with jes' a breathin' spell 'long 'bout
　　the time o' noon,
The dancers kept in motion an' the fiddle kept
　　in tune.

That picnic at Selina—it ain't to be fer-
　　got,
For a feller felt as happy's if he owned a
　　house an' lot;

An' when I think about them gals in rib-
    boned calico,
I feel like singin': "Praise the Lord from
    whom all blessin's flow!"

There'll be good times at Selina in the happy
    days to be,
But never any times like that for all the
    boys an' me,
For the mem'ry of that picnic—it'll live a
    hundred years,
An' I'll feel my old feet shufflin' when I
    climb the golden stairs!

WEARYIN' FOR YOU.

Jest a-wearyin' for you,
All the time a-feelin' blue;
Wishin' for you, wonderin' when
You'll be comin' home agen;
Restless—don't know what to do,
    Jest a-wearyin' for you.

Keep a-mopin' day by day;
Dull—in everybody's way;

Folks they smile an' pass along
Wonderin' what on earth is wrong;
'Twouldn't help 'em if they knew—
    Jest a-wearyin' for you.

Room's so lonesome, with your chair
Empty by the fireplace there;
Jest can't stand the sight of it;
Go out doors an' roam a bit,
But the woods is lonesome, too,
    Jest a-wearyin' for you.

Comes the wind with soft caress
Like the rustlin' of your dress;
Blossoms fallin' to the ground
Softly, like your footsteps sound;
Violets like your eyes so blue,
    Jest a-wearyin' for you.

Mornin' comes. The birds awake
(Use to sing so for your sake),
But there's sadness in the notes
That come thrillin' from their throats!
Seem to feel your absence, too,
    Jest a-wearyin' for you.

Evenin' comes. I miss you more
When the dark glooms in the door;

Seems jest like you orter be
There to open it for me!
Latch goes tinklin'—thrills me through—
 Sets me wearyin' for you.

Jest a-wearyin' for you!
All the time a-feelin' blue!
Wishin' for you—wonderin' when
You'll be comin' home agen.
Restless—don't know what to do—
 Jest a-wearyin' for you!

WHEN JIM WAS DEAD.

When Jim was dead—
"Hit sarved him right," the nabors sed,
An' 'bused him for the life he'd led,
An' him a-lyin' thar at rest
With not a rose upon his breast!
Ah! menny cruel words they sed
 When Jim was dead.

" Jes' killed hisself," "Too mean ter live."
They didn't hav' one word ter give
Of comfort as they hovered near
An' gazed on Jim a-lyin' there!
"Thar ain't no use to talk," they sed,
 "He's better dead."

But suddenly the room growed still,
While God's white sunshine seemed ter fill
The dark place with a gleam of life,
An' o'er the dead she bent—Jim's wife!
An' with her lips close, close ter his,
As though he knew an' felt the kiss,
She sobbed—a touchin' sight ter see—
"Ah! Jim was always good ter me!"

I tell you, when that cum ter light,
It kinder set the dead man right;
An' round the weepin' woman they
Throwed kindly arms of love that day,
An' mingled with her own they shed
The tenderest tears—when Jim was dead.

THE OLE PINE BOX.

We didn't care, in the long ago,
Fer easy-chairs 'at were made fer show—
With velvet cushions in red an' black
An' springs 'at tilted a feller back
Afore he knowed it—like them in town—
Till his heels flew up an' his hed went down!
But the seat we loved in the times of yore,
Wuz the ole pine box by the grocery store!

Thar it sot in the rain an' shine,
Four foot long by the measurin' line;
Under the chiny-berry tree—
Jes' as cozy as she could be!
Fust hedquarters fer infermation—
Best ole box in the whole creation;
Hacked an' whittled an' rote with ryme,
An' so blamed sociable all the time.

Thar we plotted an' thar we planned,
Read the news in the paper, an'
Talked o' pollyticks fur an' wide,
Got mixed up as we argyfied!
An' the ole town fiddler sawed away
At "Ole Dan Tucker" an' "Nelly Gray!"
Oh, they's boxes still—but they ain't no more
Like the ole pine box at the grocery store.

It ain't thar now, as it wuz that day—
Burnt, I reckon, or throwed away;
An' some o' the folks 'at the ole box knowed
Is fur along on the dusty road;
An' some's crost over the river wide
An' found a home on the other side.
Have they all fergot? Don't they sigh no
        more
Fer the ole pine box by the grocery store?

GOOD-BY.

There's a kind o' chilly feelin' in the blowin'
    o' the breeze,
An' a sense o' sadness stealin' through the
    tresses o' the trees;
An' it's not the sad September that's slowly
    drawin' nigh,
But jist that I remember I have come to say
    "Good-by!"

"Good-by," the wind is wailin'; "good-
    by," the trees complain,
And they bend low down to whisper with
    their green leaves white with rain;
"Good-by," the roses murmur, an' the
    bendin' lilies sigh,
As if they all felt sorry I have come to say
    "Good-by."

I reckon all have said it, some time or other
    —soft
An' easy like—with eyes cast down, that
    dared not look aloft,
For the tears that trembled in them, for the
    lips that choked the sigh—
When it kind o' took holt o' the heart, an'
    made it beat "Good-by!"

I didn't think 'twas hard to say, but stand-
      in' here alone—
With the pleasant past behin' me, an' the
      future dim, unknown,
A-gloomin' yonder in the dark, I can't keep
      back the sigh—
An' I'm weepin' like a woman, as I bid you
      all "Good-by!"

The work I've done is with you; maybe
      some things went wrong
Like a note that mars the music in the sweet
      flow of a song!
But, brethren, when you think of me, I only
      ask you would
Say as the Master said of one: "He hath
      done what he could!"

And when you sit together in the time as
      yet to be,
By your love-encircled firesides in this pleas-
      ant land of Lee,
Let the sweet past come before you, an' with
      somethin' like a sigh,
Jist say: "We ain't fergot him since the
      day he said 'Good-by!'"

OLD TIMES IN GEORGIA.

Old times in Georgy—them's the times for
me!
No times now like them times, an' never-
more will be;
Long before the railroads, an' steamers
blowin' free,
How I like to dream o' them—dear old times
to me!

Old times in Georgy—them's the times that
make
My old eyes shine like sunlight on some
sweet mountain lake;
An' sometimes, too, they kinder bring
feelin's full o' pain,
An' make my eyes run over, like rivers
swelled by rain!

Old times in Georgy—I can't forget 'em
quite,
Suns that made the daytime, stars that made
the night;
Wasn't they jest splendid—didn't they shine
bright?
All the world was love then, all the world
was light!

7

Old times in Georgy—hear my old heart beat
When they come a-ringin' with their music
    sweet!
Dreamin' of 'em always, here where Mem'ry
    dwells,
They're like a sweet song's echo—a far-off
    chime o' bells!

Old times in Georgy, they was sweet to
    know—
Old fren's that loved us, fren's that we loved
    so!
Seem to lost my way, now—ain't much left
    to see—
Them dear old times in Georgy is all life has
    for me!

THE LAZY MAN.

I'm the laziest man, I reckon, that a mortal
    ever seed!
Got money? Nary dollar! I wasn't built
    fer greed,
Fer graspin' an' fer gripin' where the rev-
    enue is found;
I'm what you call a lazy 'un—jes' built fer
    lyin' round!

Contented? Mighty right I am; when spring
  winds whistle sweet
In the meadows where the daisies make a
  carpet fer your feet;
Where the nestin' birds are chirpin'; where
  the brook, in witchin' play,
Goes laughin' on, a-pushin' all the lilies out
  his way,
You'll find me almost any time a-lyin' at
  my ease
With the lull song o' the locust an' the
  drowsy drone o' bees
Above me an' aroun' me. I'm a poet in my
  way,
An' I'd rather hear the birds sing than to
  shoot 'em any day!
"Jes' laziness," they tell me, an' I reckon
  they are right;
But the world's so full o' beauty, an' you
  can't see much at night!
But different folks has different minds, nor
  drink from the same cup;
When I'm laughin' with the lilies, they're
  a-plowin' of 'em up.

My field's a pasture fer the cows, an' though
  it never pays,
It's a powerful source o' pleasure jes' ter see
  the creeturs graze!

The tinkle, tinkle o' the bells is such a pleasin'
    sound—
But I'm a lazy chap, you know, jes' built
    fer lyin' round!

DIDN'T THINK O' LOSIN' HIM.

Always wuz abusin' him—
Rough an' rougher usin' him,
Love an' all refusin' him,
    Though his tears 'ud fall;
Didn't think o' losin' him—
    Not at all!

He, poor feller, he'd just sigh,
With a waterin' o' the eye—
Say: "It's all my fault," an' try
    T' stave 'em off awhile!
"Some day I'll lay down an' die—
    Then they'll smile."

An' he did. God's sometimes heap
Kinder ter His poor lost sheep
Than the ones 'at has their keep;
    So, one darkened day,
He jest told him, "Go to sleep,"
    In His own kind way.

Then the poor, sad, tearful eyes
Smiled their thanks ter God's own skies
With a kind o' sweet surprise—
    And the heart growed still.
Said one of 'em: "Thar he lies;
    'Tis God's will!"

.   .   .   .

Always wuz abusin' him—
Rough an' rougher usin' him,
Love an' all refusin' him,
    Though his tears 'ud fall;
Didn't think o' losin' him—
    Not at all!

———

THE LIGHTNING AGE.

What's the world a-comin' to, a feller'd like
    to know,
When they're makin' ice to order an' man-
    ufacturin' snow?
An' now, as if to vex us, another thing we
    hear:
They're makin' rain in Texas without a word
    o' prayer!

The cities—they're gone out o' sight; it
    'pears jes' like a dream,
For when they have a cloudy night they run
    the stars by steam!
And here's the lightnin', with a song, pro-
    claimin' man is boss,
An' all the street cars skimmin' 'long with-
    out a mule or hoss!

An' here's that ringin' telephone, which
    never seems to tire,
But takes a man's voice, free o' charge, across
    six mile o' wire;
An' here's the blessed phonygraf, which
    makes your memory vain,
An', like a woman, when you talk, keeps
    talkin' back again!

Lord! how the world is movin' on, beneath
    the sun an' moon!
I can't help thinkin' I was born a hundred
    years too soon;
But when I go—praise be to God!—it won't
    be in the night,
For my grave will shine like glory in a
    bright electric light!

"SHOUTIN'."

There's lots an' lots of people (if you'll jes'
    believe my song)
What says we shoutin' Methodists has got
    the business wrong.
Well, they're welcome to their 'pinions, but
    of one thing I'm secure:
If they ever git religion they will shout a
    hundred sure!

I was once into a love-feast, an' talk of
    shoutin'—why,
It almost shook the windows in the everlast-
    in' sky!
An' the Presbyterian people, they were happy
    —not a few—
An' the Baptist brother come along an' jined
    the shoutin', too.

I tell you, folks, religion is a curious kind o'
    thing;
It gives a man a heart to pray—a powerful
    voice to sing!
An' if you've only got it—though there ain't
    no shoutin' heard—
The people's bound to know it if you never
    say a word!

We're sailin' in the same old ship—no mat-
    ter where we roam;
The Baptists an' the Methodists—we're all
    a-goin' home:
An' no matter how we travel, by our differ-
    ent creeds enticed,
We'll all git home together if we're only
    one in Christ!

The paths we tread are sometimes rough,
    an' flowerless is the sod;
"This world is not a friend of grace to help
    us on to God!"
But the lights o' Canaan shinin' o'er the
    river's crystal tide,
Seem to woo us to the city that is on the
    other side!

Then let us sing together, for we're bound
    to git thar soon,
"On the Other Side of Jordan" (will some
    brother raise the tune?)
"Where the tree of life is bloomin'," sheddin'
    blossoms o'er the foam,
"There is rest for all the weary;" an' we're
    goin', goin' home.

JONES' COTTON PLANTER.

He ain't of no account at all, jes' giv' up
    everything
For what he calls "inventin'," bin a-foolin'
    'long sence spring
With a queer kin' o' contraption which has
    turned that head o' his;
Calls it "Jones' Cotton Planter," but the Lord
    knows what it is!

He took it to the city, showed it to the board
    o' trade,
An' they thought it was amazin' an' said:
    "Jones, your fortun's made!"
I know they wuz a-foolin' him—got lots of
    imperdence!
But he cum home highfalutin', an' he hain't
    knowed nuthin' sence.

He's built himself a blacksmith shop, an'
    thar he works away,
With the pesky bellows roarin' like a cyclone
    night an' day;
Ain't reg'lar at his meals no more, man of
    a fam'ly, too;
I wish that cotton planter was in—Georgy,
    so I do!

It strikes me they've got things enough
    without his makin' more,
Unless he fixed up somethin' for the grass
    that's at his door;
But the cotton planter's got him, an' the
    children's worked to death,
For he keeps em' at the bellows till they're
    almost out o' breath.

Sich a blowin', sich a hammerin', sich a
    sawin'—never stops;
Can't git him interested in the weather or
    the crops.
"I'm a gittin' thar!" he'll tell you; "she'll
    be ready by the fall;
And Jones' cotton planter'll take the shine
    from off 'em all!"

He's done fur.   No use talkin'; he's a
    ruined man as sure
As Betsy, thar, is sittin' with her knittin' at
    the door;
Alas! for all the children—they'll be down to
    skin and bones,
An' ones' cotton planter'll be the epitaph
    o' Jones!

www.ingramcontent.com/pod-product-compliance
Lightning Source LLC
Chambersburg PA
CBHW020803020726
47495CB00008B/2563